∤
E
M145p

# Puzzlers

# Puzzlers

## Bill Oakes
## Suse MacDonald

Dial Books for Young Readers * New York

To thinking in new ways
—B.O. and S.M.

Published by Dial Books for Young Readers
A Division of Penguin Books USA Inc.
2 Park Avenue, New York, New York 10016
Published simultaneously in Canada
by Fitzhenry & Whiteside Limited, Toronto
Copyright © 1989 by Suse MacDonald and Bill Oakes
All rights reserved
Designed by the authors
Typography by the authors and Amelia Lau Carling
Printed in the U.S.A.
E
First Edition
10 9 8 7 6 5 4 3 2 1

Library of Congress Cataloging in Publication Data
MacDonald, Suse. Puzzlers.
Summary: An introduction to elementary concepts such
as "widest," "tallest," and "back-to-back," where the
reader is asked to pick out the number with that
quality in an animal that is made up of numbers.
1. Art—Themes, motives—Juvenile literature.
2. Picture puzzles—Juvenile literature.
3. Numbers, Natural, in art—Juvenile literature.
[1. Numbers, Natural. 2. Counting. 3. Picture puzzles.]
I. Oakes, Bill. II. Title.
N7440.M34 1989   [E]   88-33392
ISBN 0-8037-0689-8
ISBN 0-8037-0690-1 (lib. bdg.)

The full-color artwork was created by cutting shapes
from hand-textured paper and applying them to a plain,
colored background. It was then color-separated
and reproduced as red, blue, yellow, and black halftones.

This book is filled with a colorful parade of animals: a rooster, a frog, a beaver, a peacock, and lots more. But if you look closely, you'll find that these animals are special—they're made up of numbers. And the numbers are playing games of their own. Some are bulging at the sides, trying to be the widest number in the group. Some are stretching to be the tallest. Others have tumbled upside down or lined up back-to-back, and they're all having fun.

See if you can find the widest number in the duck, and the tallest number in the toucan. The numbers in the small squares facing each picture will show you what to look for.

Once you've solved all the Puzzlers, go back and see how many other games you can find in each picture. Which is the tallest number in the duck? Are any numbers upside down in the toucan?

An *Answers* section at the back lists the games we think you can find, but these numbers are so playful, you may even notice ones we missed! Good luck!

widest

Find the widest number ➔

tallest

Find the tallest number ➜

backward

 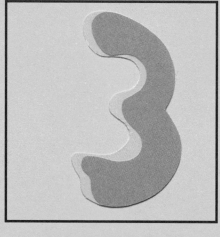 

Find the backward number ⇨

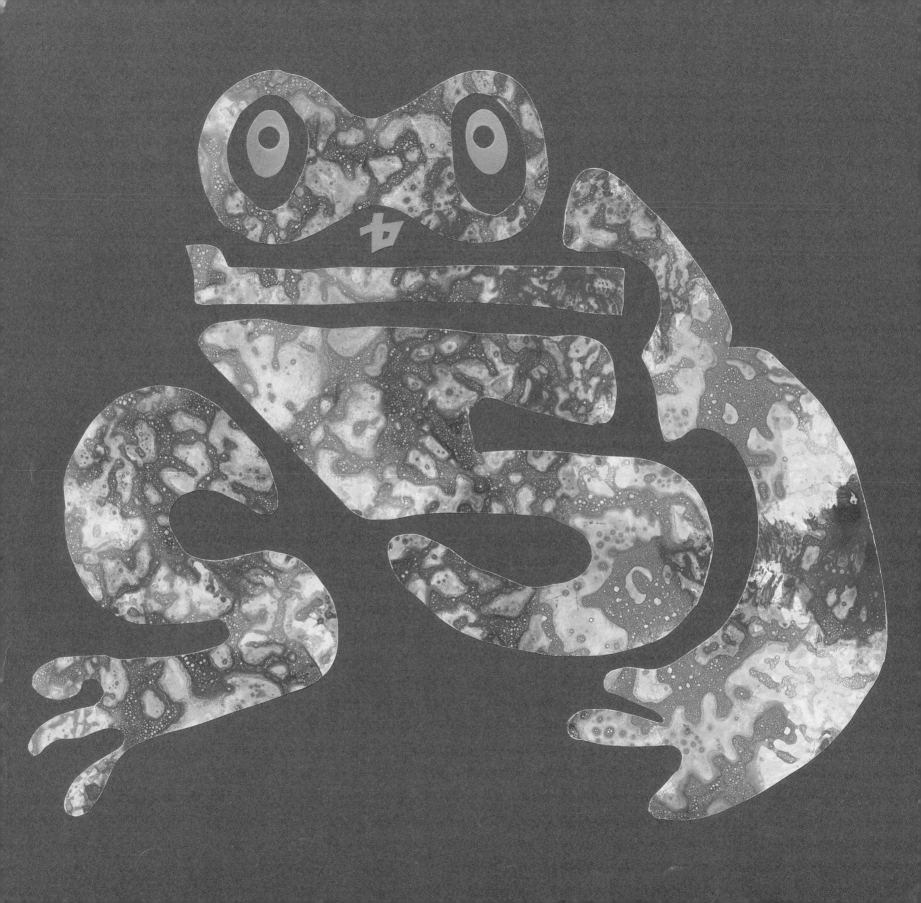

# upside down

Find the upside-down number ⇨

pair

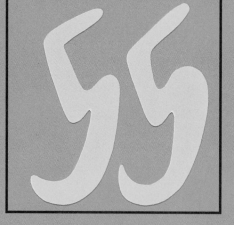

Find the pair of numbers ➔

# back-to-back

Find the back-to-back numbers ⇨

facing

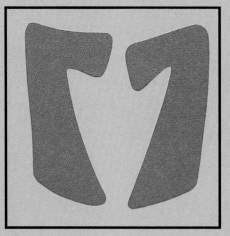

Find the facing numbers ⇾

pattern

 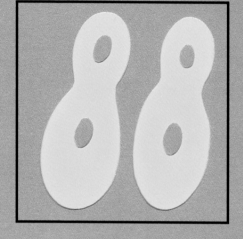 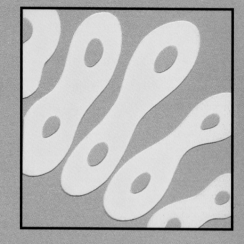

Find the pattern of numbers →

Find the overlapping numbers ⇨

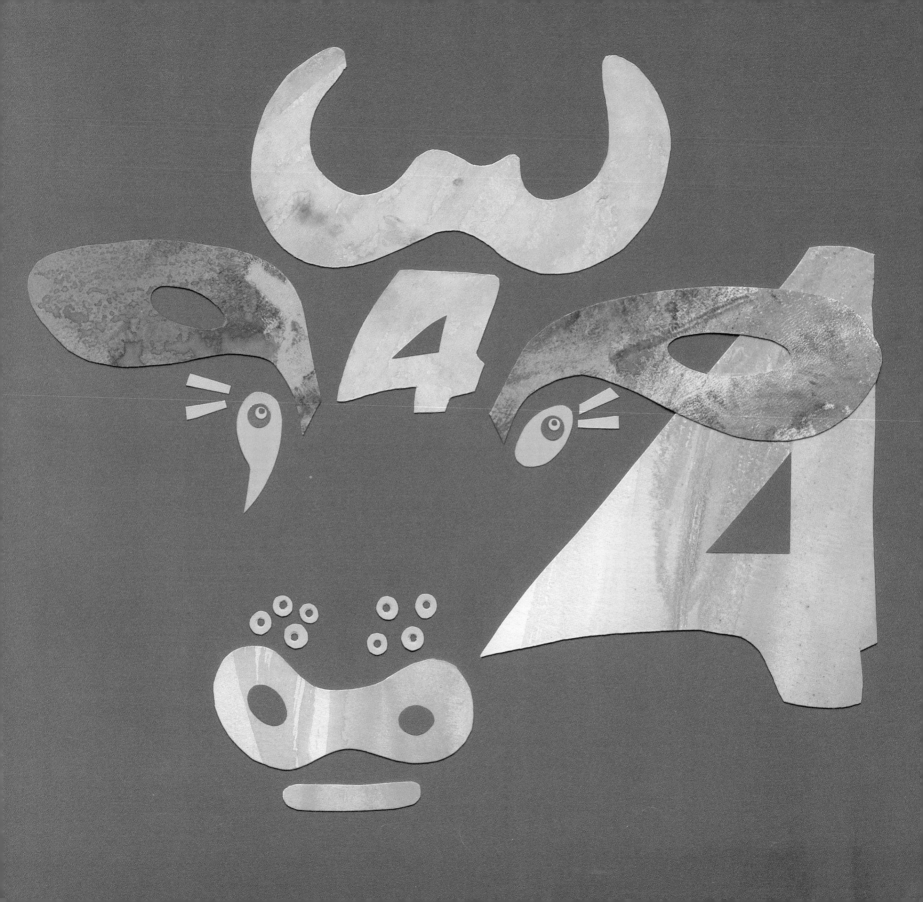

# sequence

 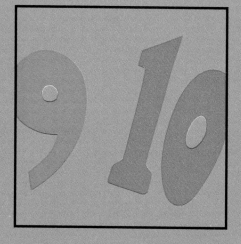 

**Find the sequence of numbers** ⇨

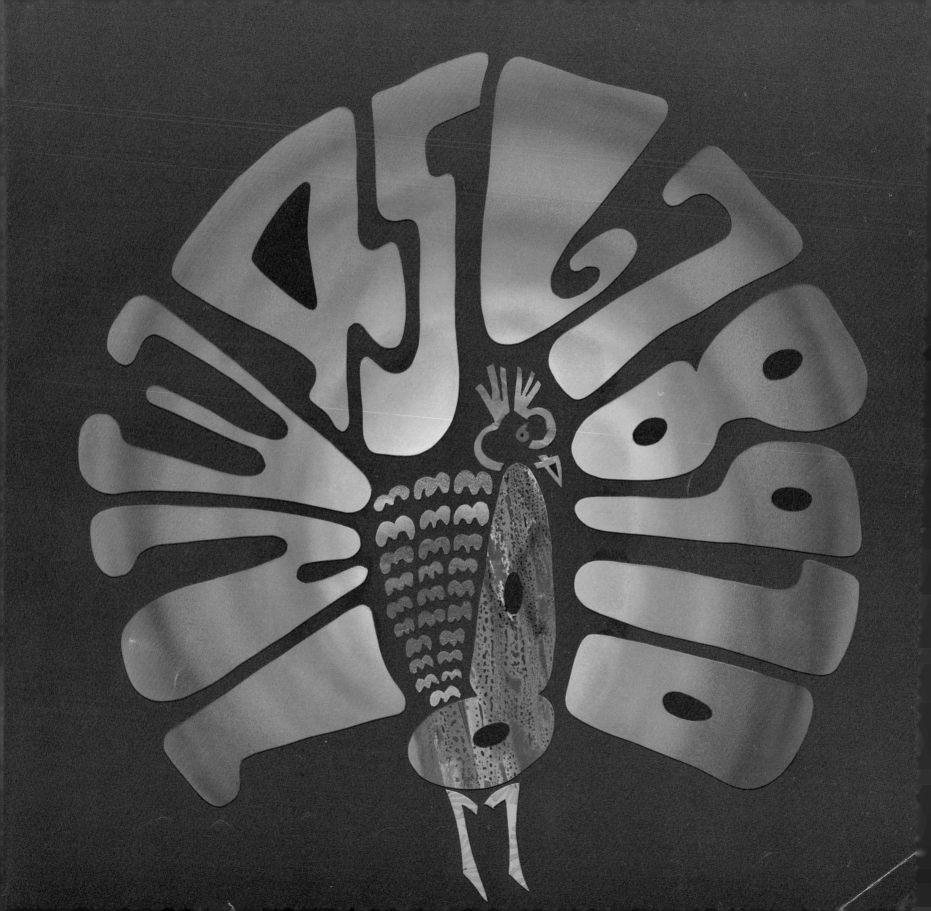

What can you find in the crazy creature? ⇨

Find the widest number,
the tallest number,
the backward number,
the upside-down number,
the pair of numbers,
the back-to-back numbers,
the facing numbers,
the pattern of numbers,
the overlapping numbers,
the sequence of numbers.

# Answers to the Puzzlers

1 The *five* that forms the Duck's body is its **widest** part.

3 The *two* that forms one of the Frog's legs is **backward.**

2 The *three* that forms the Toucan's body is its **tallest** part.

4 The *five* that forms the Beaver's ear is **upside down.**

5 The *twos* that form the Rooster's feet are a **pair.**

6 The *fours* that form the Pig's ears are **back-to-back.**

7 The *sevens* that form the Monkey's shoulders and the *nines* that form his ears are **facing** each other.

8 The *sevens* that form the Fish's top fin are a **pattern.**

9 The *nine* that forms the Cow's ear **overlaps** with the *four* that forms her neck.

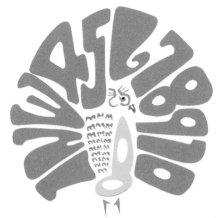

10 The numbers *one* to *ten* that form the Peacock's tail are a **sequence.**

The **widest** and **tallest** part of this creature is the *five* that forms its body. Its foot is a **backward** *two*. The *four* on the creature's forehead is **upside down**. A **pair** of *sevens* form wings near the creature's tail. **Back-to-back** *fours* make up two of the creature's beaks, while two *nines* that are **facing** each other form its ears. A **pattern** of *sevens* are the creature's leg hairs. The *three* that forms its front wing, the *twos* that are its feet, and the *sevens* that form its rear wings all **overlap** with the *five* that forms the creature's body. The tail is made up of a **sequence** of *one, two,* and *three*.

---

## Other games you can find in each Puzzler

| | | |
|---|---|---|
| 1 Duck | Tallest | *Five* (body) |
| | Backward | *Three* (head) |
| | Pattern | *Sevens* (tail) |
| | | |
| 2 Toucan | Overlap | *Nine* (eye) and *Three* (body) |
| | | |
| 3 Frog | Widest | *One* (mouth) |
| | Tallest | *Three* (leg) |
| | Upside down | *Four* (nose) |
| | Pairs | *Zeros* (eyes) |
| | | |
| 4 Beaver | Widest | *Nine* (tail) |
| | Tallest | *Nine* (tail) |
| | Backward | *Nine* (tail) |
| | Overlap | *Zero* (eye) and *Two* (face) |
| | | |
| 5 Rooster | Widest | *Three* (body) |
| | Tallest | *Three* (tail) |
| | Backward | *Three* (neck) |
| | Facing | *Threes* (neck) |
| | Sequence | *One, Two, Three* (tail) |
| | | |
| 6 Pig | Widest | *Three* (head) |
| | Tallest | *Three* (head) |
| | Backward | *Four* (ear), *Two* (eye) |
| | Pairs | *Fours* (ear), *Twos* and *Zeros* (eyes), *Ones* (eyelashes) |
| | Overlap | *Three* (head/chin) and *Four* (ear) |

| | | |
|---|---|---|
| 7 Monkey | Widest | *Three* (head) |
| | Tallest | *Seven* (shoulder) |
| | Backward | *Nine* (ear) |
| | Upside down | *Sixes* (eyes) |
| | Pairs | *Sixes* and *Zeros* (eyes), *Nines* (ears), *Sevens* (shoulders) |
| | | |
| 8 Fish | Widest | *Three* (tail) |
| | Tallest | *Three* (tail) |
| | Backward | *Three* (tail) |
| | Upside down | *Sevens* (top fin) |
| | Pair | *Zeros* (bottom fins) |
| | Overlap | *Three* (middle fin) and *Five* (body) *Three* (middle fin) and *Zero* (bottom fin) |
| | | |
| 9 Cow | Widest | *Four* (neck) |
| | Tallest | *Four* (neck) |
| | Backward | *Nine* (ear) |
| | Pairs | *Nines* (ears), *Ones* (eyelashes) |
| | Back-to-back | *Nines* (ears) |
| | Pattern | *Zeros* (spots on nose) |
| | | |
| 10 Peacock | Widest | *Four* (tail) |
| | Tallest | *Five* (tail) |
| | Backward | *Five* (head) |
| | Upside down | *Four* (beak), *Nine* (eye) |
| | Pairs | *Fives* (head), *Sevens* (legs) |
| | Back-to-back | *Fives* (head) |
| | Pattern | *Threes* (tail design) |